The Magic Raincoat

For Emily: though your magic raincoat grows old and dusty, and pale and permeable, may it never lose its magic or cease to inspire your delicate heart
—R.D.

To my mum and dad. Thank you for my mischievous childhood.
—S.B.

# The **Magic** Raincoat

## Ryan **David**

**ILLUSTRATIONS BY**
Sibylla **Benatova**

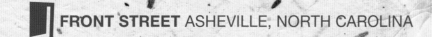
**FRONT STREET** ASHEVILLE, NORTH CAROLINA

Emily got a new raincoat.
It was bright orange
and it had clasps and buttons
and zippers and straps
and buckles and at least
seven pockets.

But she was mad

because she had asked for a **yellow** raincoat.

When Emily put it on, it didn't fit.

It was **way** too **big**!

So she yelled, "I **wish** it **fit** me!" Her mama turned around and said, "That fits you **perfectly**, dear."

Sure enough, the coat had become
smaller and smaller until it fit her perfectly.
Emily blinked in surprise and thought,
"There must be something special
about this raincoat!"

So she decided
to wear it all day.

Later on, her little brother was playing with **her doll,** so she stamped her foot and yelled, "I wish you were …

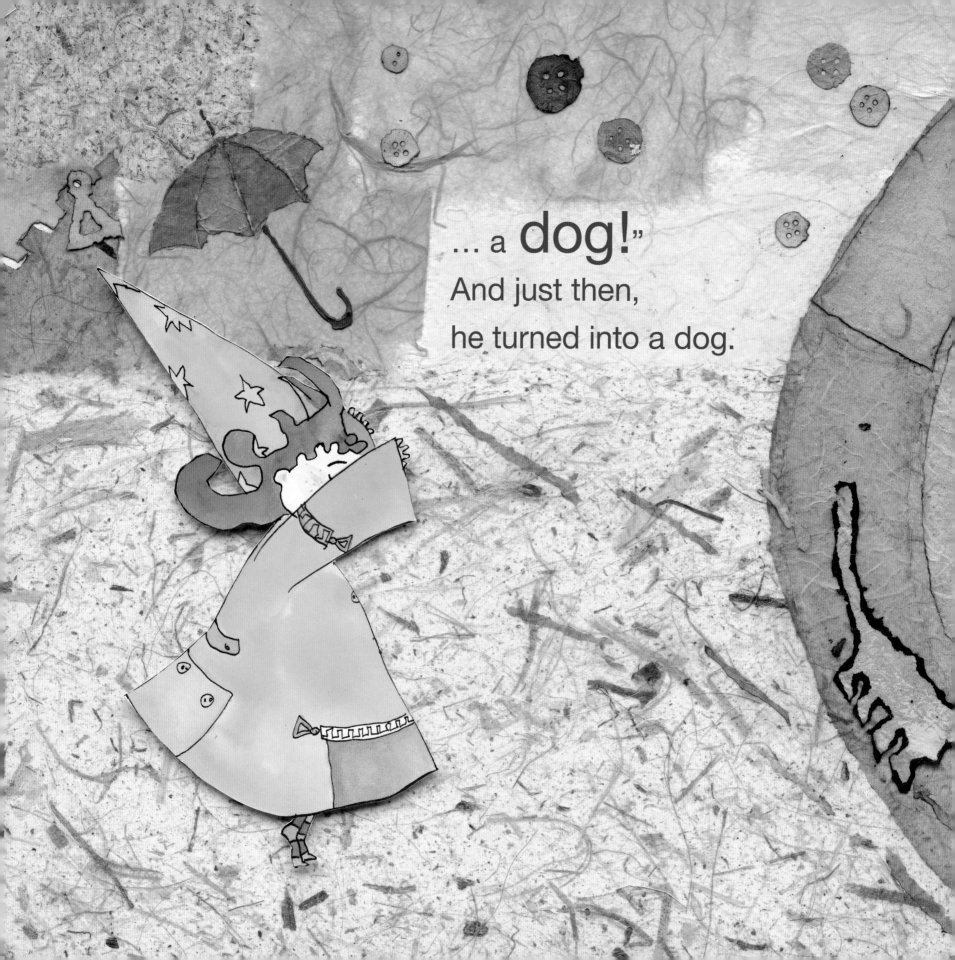

... a **dog!**"
And just then,
he turned into a dog.

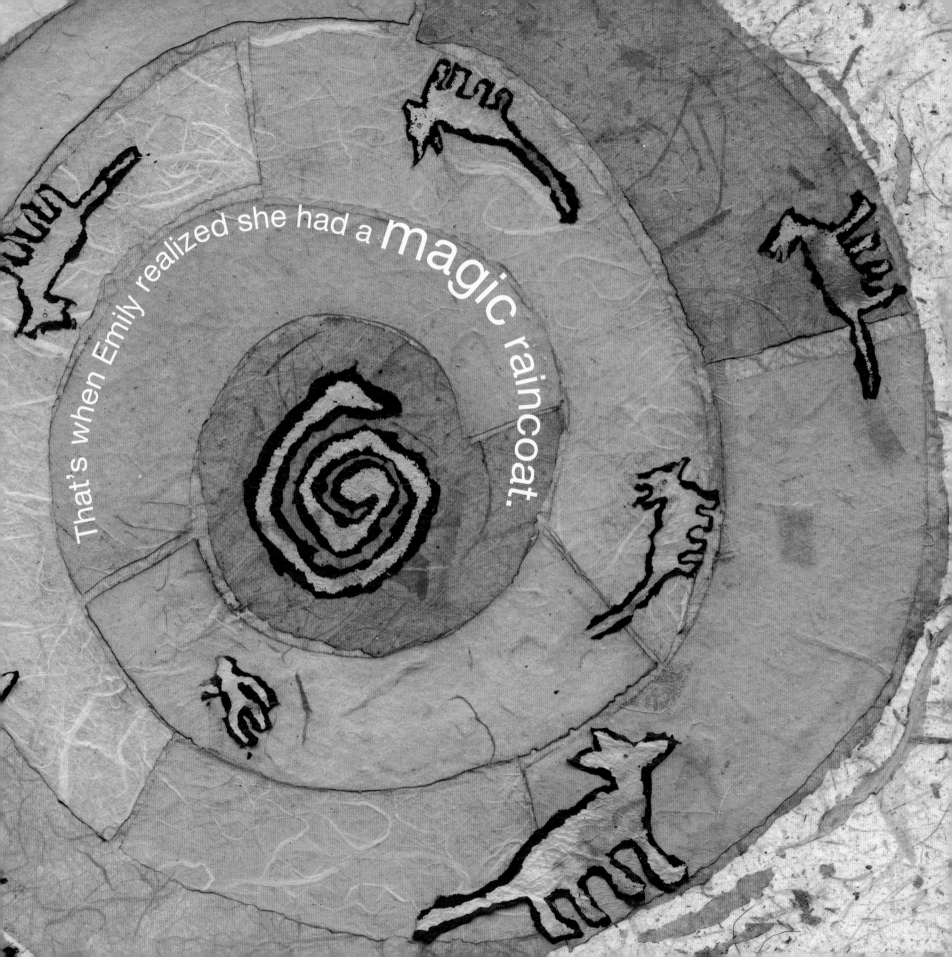

That's when Emily realized she had a magic raincoat.

So she tightened the **clasps**,
buttoned the **buttons**,
zipped the **zippers**,
tied the **straps**,

She carried the
briefcase to
her room and said,
"I wish I had
a **purple** gorilla!"

Just then a truck pulled up the driveway
and out stepped a gorilla
dressed in a fine purple silk robe

and carrying a **purple** umbrella.

So Emily said,
"I wish **Daddy** were
HOME all the time!"

And her daddy came home from work,
shaking his head and sighing,

"Would you believe my
boss just fired me!"

Mama was very sad,

and they ate plain pasta for dinner that nigh

and **burnt** cookies for dessert.

Emily decided right then that she would

use her magic raincoat only for GOOD causes.

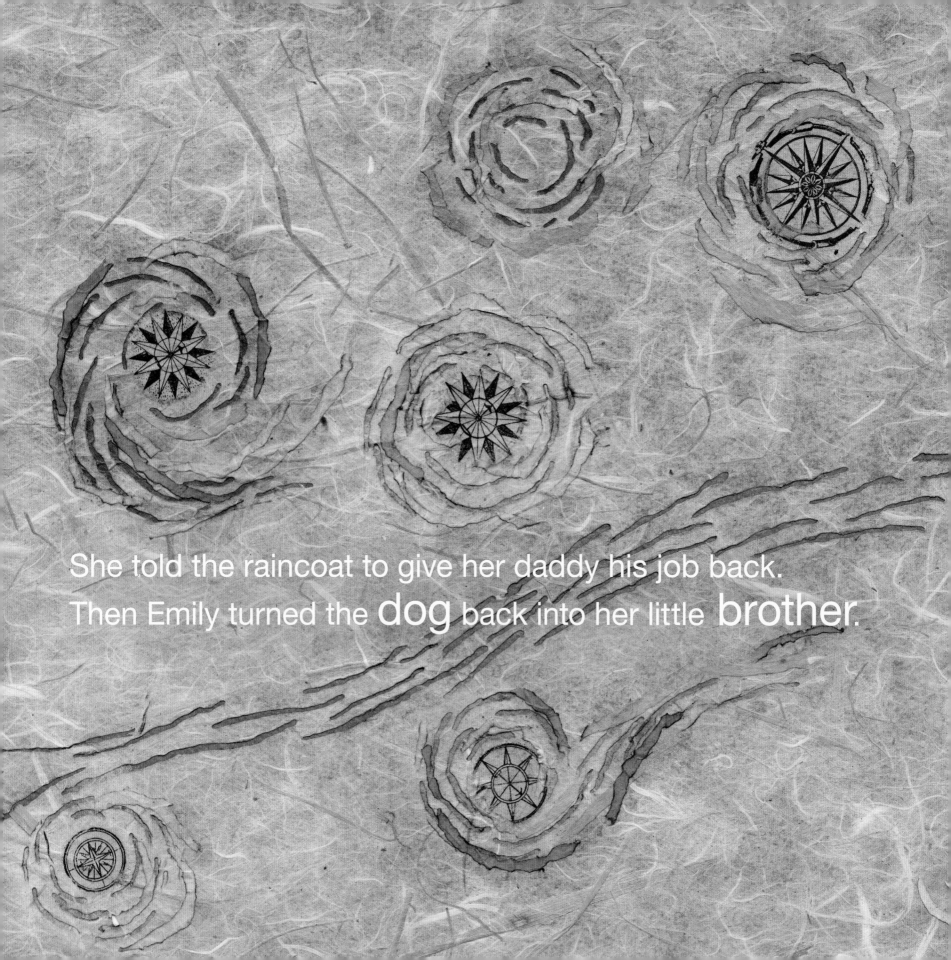

She told the raincoat to give her daddy his job back.
Then Emily turned the dog back into her little brother.

She **slept** well that night, dreaming of flying **ice-cream** cones and warm blackberry pie with **chocolate** sauce.

But the next morning, her raincoat was **gone.**

"Where's my raincoat?" Emily asked.
Her mama smiled, took out a
new yellow raincoat, and said,

"You wanted a yellow one, and our neighbor's girl, Mei, wanted an orange one, so I traded with Mei's mother last night."

Just then Emily looked out the window and saw the neighbors' car turn into a boat

"I've got to **stop** that raincoat," thought Emily.

But by the time Emily arrived at Mei's house, Mei had already turned her little brother into a **penguin**.

So Emily explained that it was a **magic** raincoat, and she and Mei agreed that magic raincoats were too special to wear all day.

Emily gave Mei the **yellow** raincoat and changed Mei's penguin back into her little brother.

Then Emily carried

the **orange** raincoat

home.

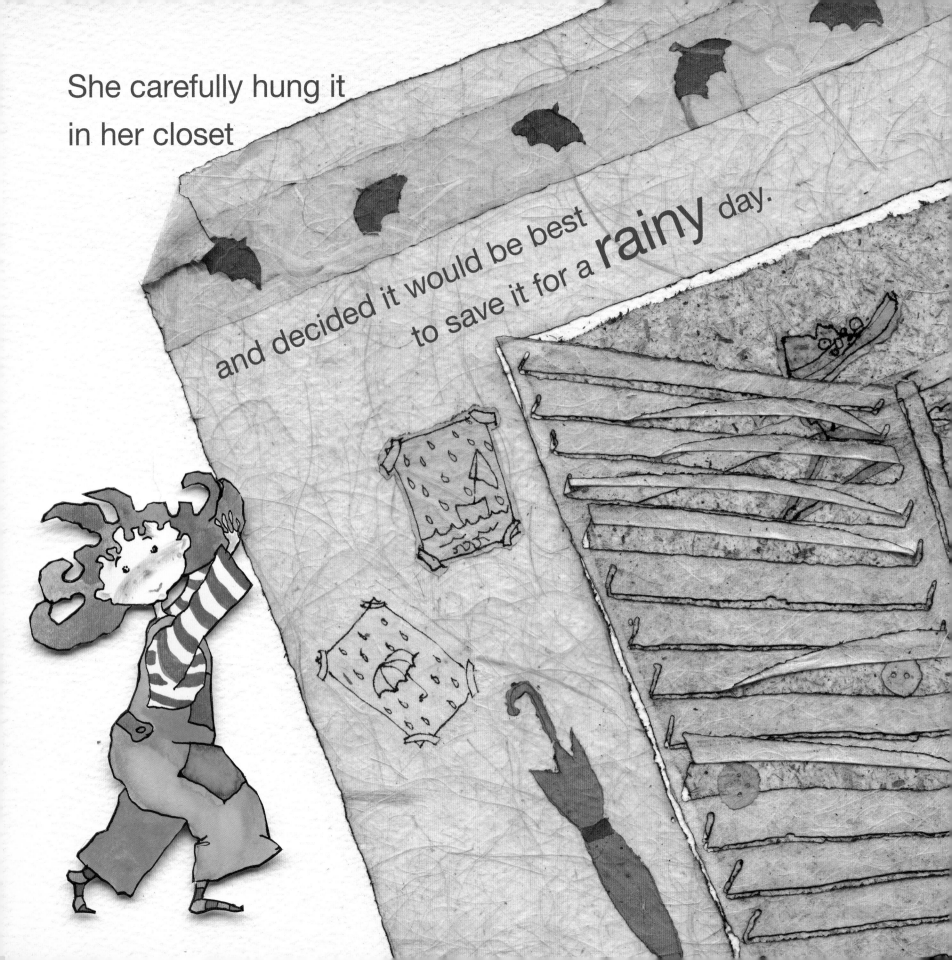

She carefully hung it
in her closet

and decided it would be best
to save it for a rainy day.

magic
box

E

Library of Congress Cataloging-in-Publication Data

David, Ryan.
The magic raincoat / Ryan David ;
illustrations by Sibylla Benatova.—1st ed.
p. cm.
Summary: Emily is not happy with her new raincoat until she
discovers that it is magical, so when her mother trades it to the
neighbor who was equally unhappy with her own new raincoat,
Emily must think of a way to trade back.
ISBN-13: 978-1-932425-68-0
(hardcover : alk. paper)
[1. Raincoats—Fiction. 2. Magic—Fiction.]
I. Shekerdjiska-Benatova, Sibylla, ill. II. Title.
PZ7.D282334Mag 2007
[E]—dc22
2006011726

FRONT STREET
An Imprint of Boyds Mills Press, Inc.
A Highlights Company

815 Church Street
Honesdale, Pennsylvania 18431